BLACKBERRY FARM

CHRISTMAS AT BLACKBERRY FARM

Jane Pilgrim

This edition first published in the United Kingdom in 2000 by
Brockhampton Press
20 Bloomsbury Street
London WC1B 3QA
a member of the Caxton Publishing Group

© Text copyright MCMLII by Jane Pilgrim
© Illustrations copyright MCMLII by Hodder & Stoughton Ltd

Designed and Produced for Brockhampton Press by
Open Door Limited
80 High Street, Colsterworth, Lincolnshire, NG33 5JA

Illustrator: F. Stocks May
Colour separation: GA Graphics Stamford

Title: BLACKBERRY FARM, Christmas at Blackberry Farm
ISBN: 1-84186-066-2

CHRISTMAS AT BLACKBERRY FARM

Jane Pilgrim

Illustrated by F. Stocks May

BROCKHAMPTON PRESS

On Christmas Eve at Blackberry Farm the moon was bright and the stars were twinkling, and the light from the kitchen window shone out across the snowy yard. The animals waited excitedly for Mrs Smiles, the farmer's wife, to call them in.

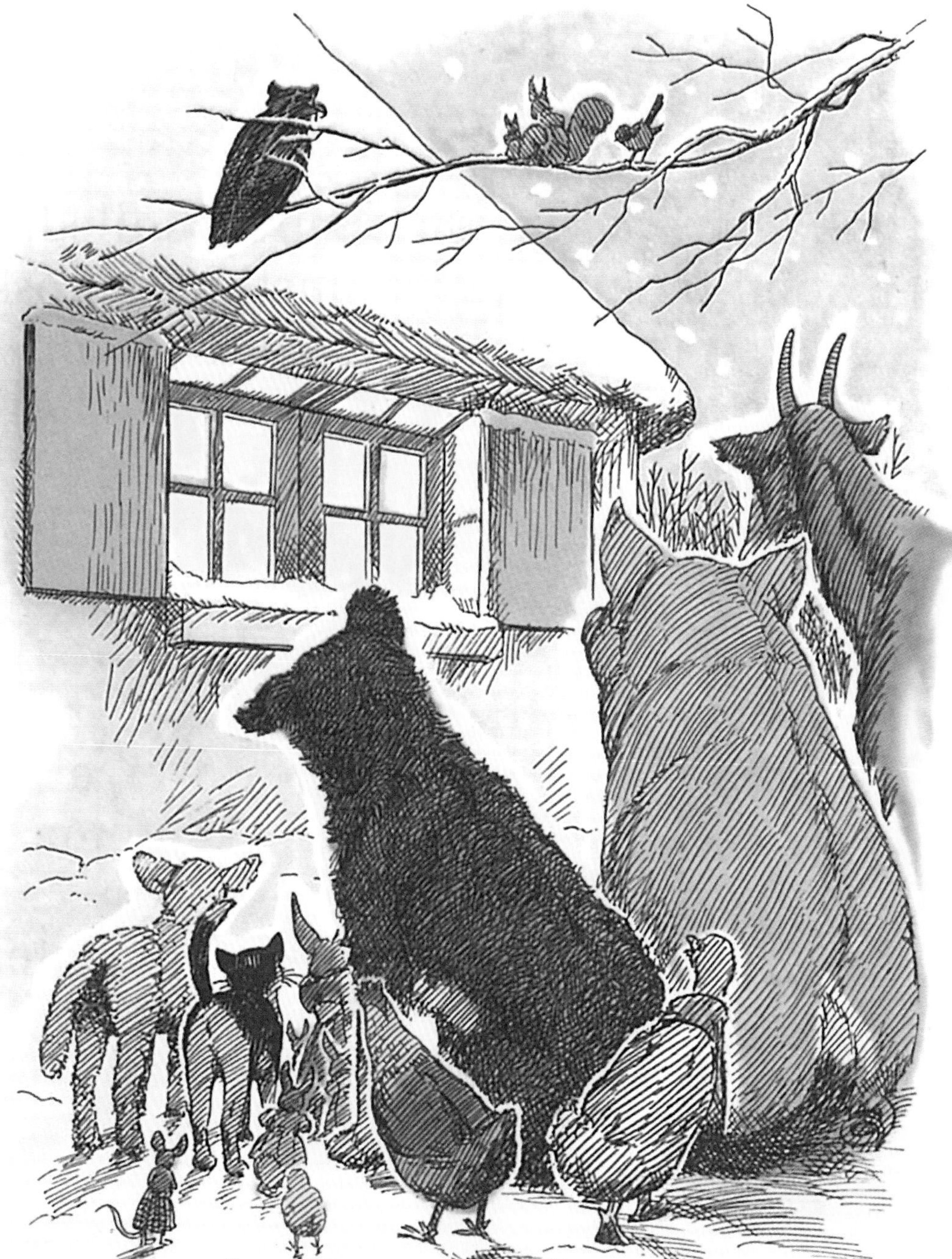

At six o'clock Mrs Smiles called, and they all came hustling across the yard. First, Rusty the Sheepdog, Ernest Owl, and George the Kitten. Mother Hen and Mary, Walter Duck, Lucy Mouse, Emily the Goat, and Little Martha the Lamb followed. Scuttling beside them were Mrs Squirrel and Hazel, and Mrs Nibble, with her three babies. Last, but not least, came Henry the Pig, with Joe Robin begging him to hurry lest he be late.

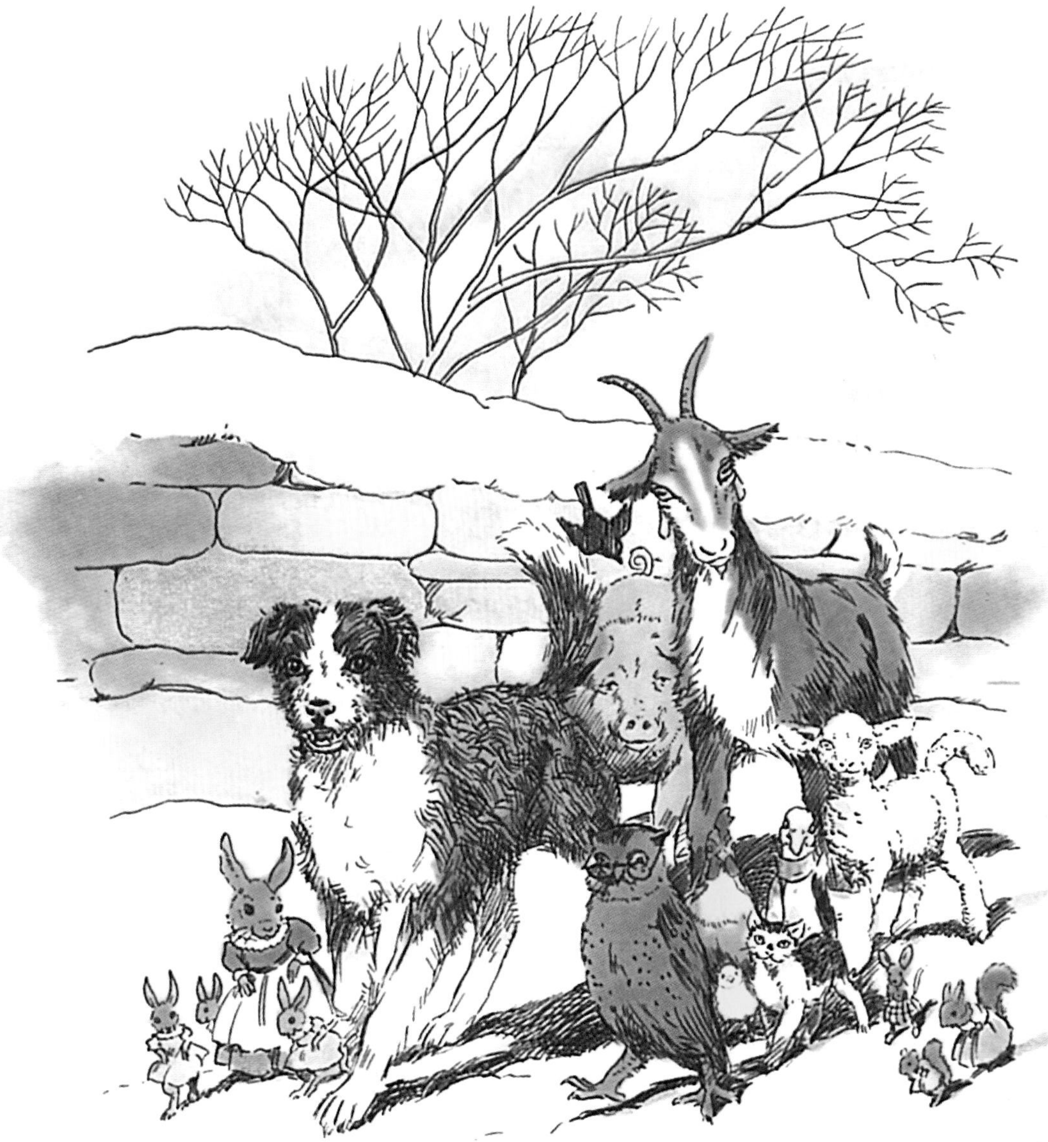

And waiting for them all in the kitchen were Mr and Mrs Smiles with their children, Joy and Bob.

"Come in, come in!" cried Mrs Smiles. "Father Christmas is coming to-night, and you must all hang up your stockings before you go to bed.

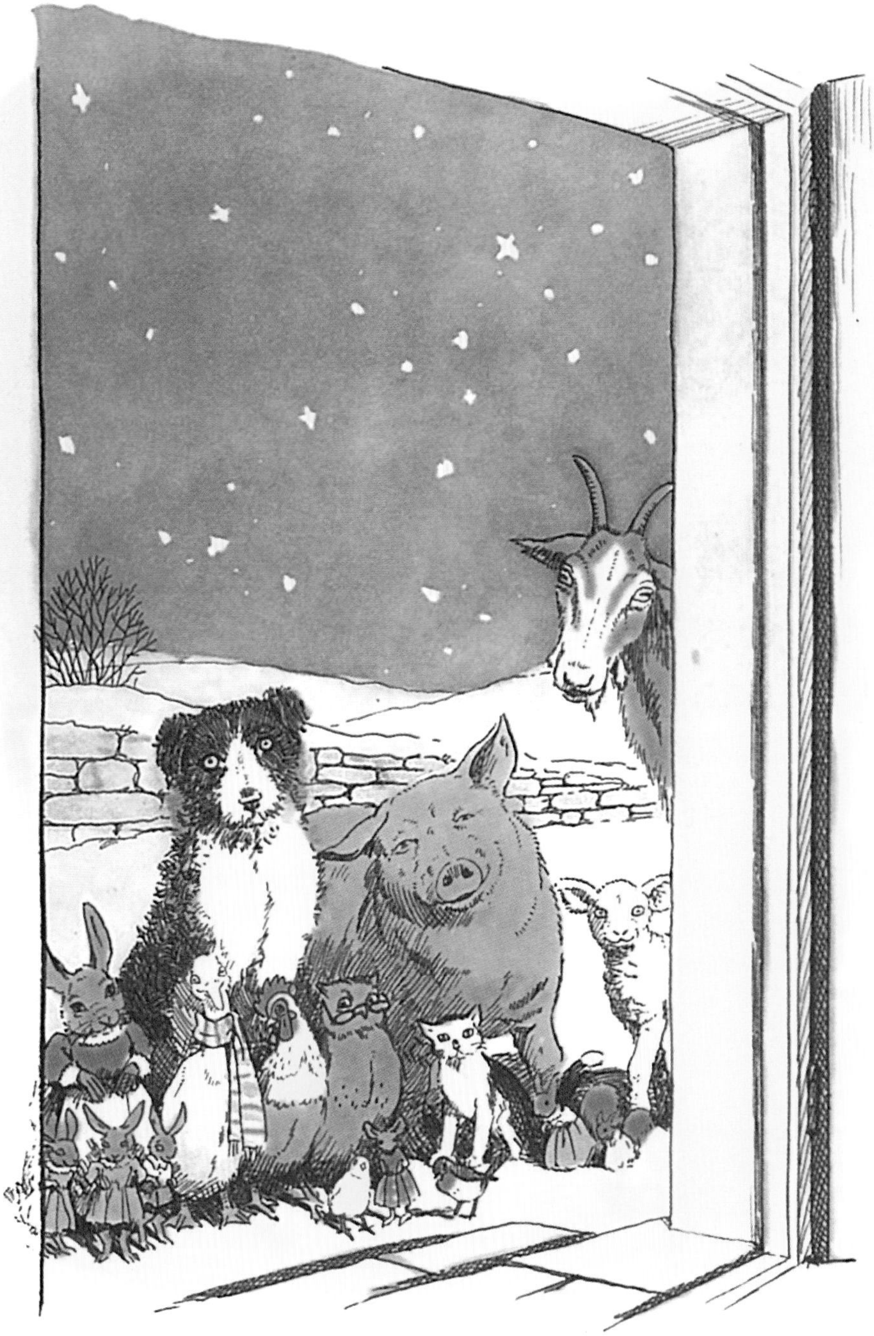

There were three LARGE
stockings: one for Emily, one for
Henry, and one for Rusty.
There were nine MIDDLE-SIZED
stockings: one for Joy and one for
Bob, one for Mrs Nibble and one
for Little Martha, one for Ernest
Owl and one for Walter Duck, one
for Mother Hen, one for George,
and one for Mrs Squirrel.

And there were seven SMALL stockings: one each for the three little Bunnies, one each for Mary Hen and Joe Robin, and one each for Lucy Mouse and little Hazel the Squirrel.

Bob handed them out, and
Ernest Owl had to speak sharply
to George the Kitten, who tried to
get a large stocking instead of a
middle-sized one.

Then they all hung them up on a line in front of the kitchen chimney: Lucy Mouse first, because she was the smallest, and Henry the Pig last, because he was the biggest. And they said good night to each other and all went off to bed, leaving Mr and Mrs Smiles sitting beside the fire thinking what a lovely large family they had at Blackberry Farm.

The next morning was
Christmas Day, and everyone was
awake very early. When Joy and
Bob rushed out across the yard
before breakfast, they could hear
all the animals chattering
excitedly. "Happy Christmas,
everyone!" called Joy and Bob.
"Happy Christmas!" called back
all the animals, and they came
bouncing over the snow to the
farm door as soon as they were
let out, longing to see what was
inside their stockings.

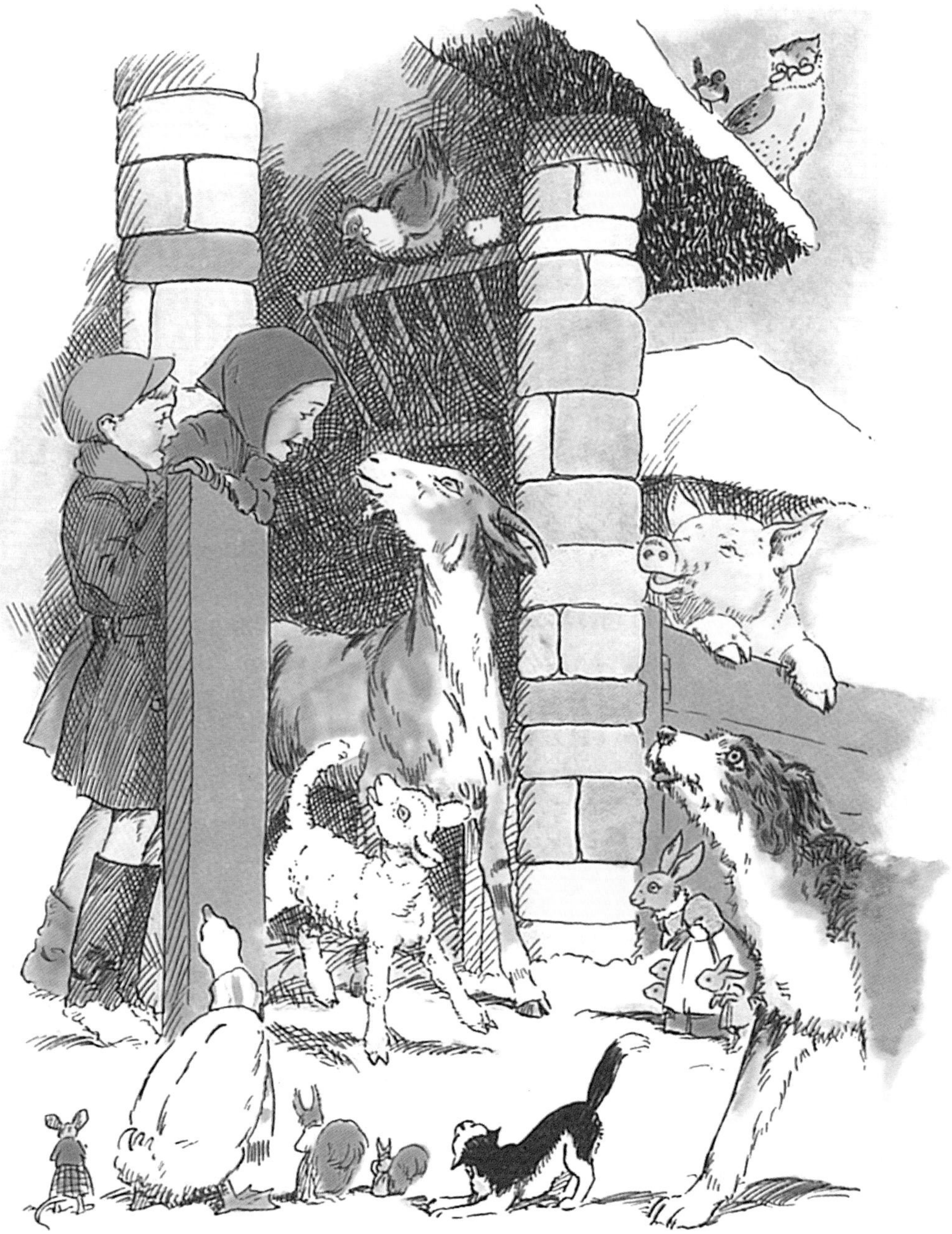

How exciting it all was! The
stockings were bulging with
lovely things. Rusty had a
beautiful, big bone. Ernest Owl
had a large new pencil-box, and
the three little Bunnies each had a
new bib and a new mug. Everyone
had something nice, and they
were all very, very happy, and
went off to have their breakfast
clutching their new treasures.

Mrs Smiles had not enough room
for everyone in the kitchen for
Christmas dinner, so the animals
had theirs round a large wooden
table in the barn. Ernest Owl sat
at one end and Henry the Pig at
the other. They had a large
Christmas pudding, lots of
mincepies, and plenty of paper
hats and crackers.

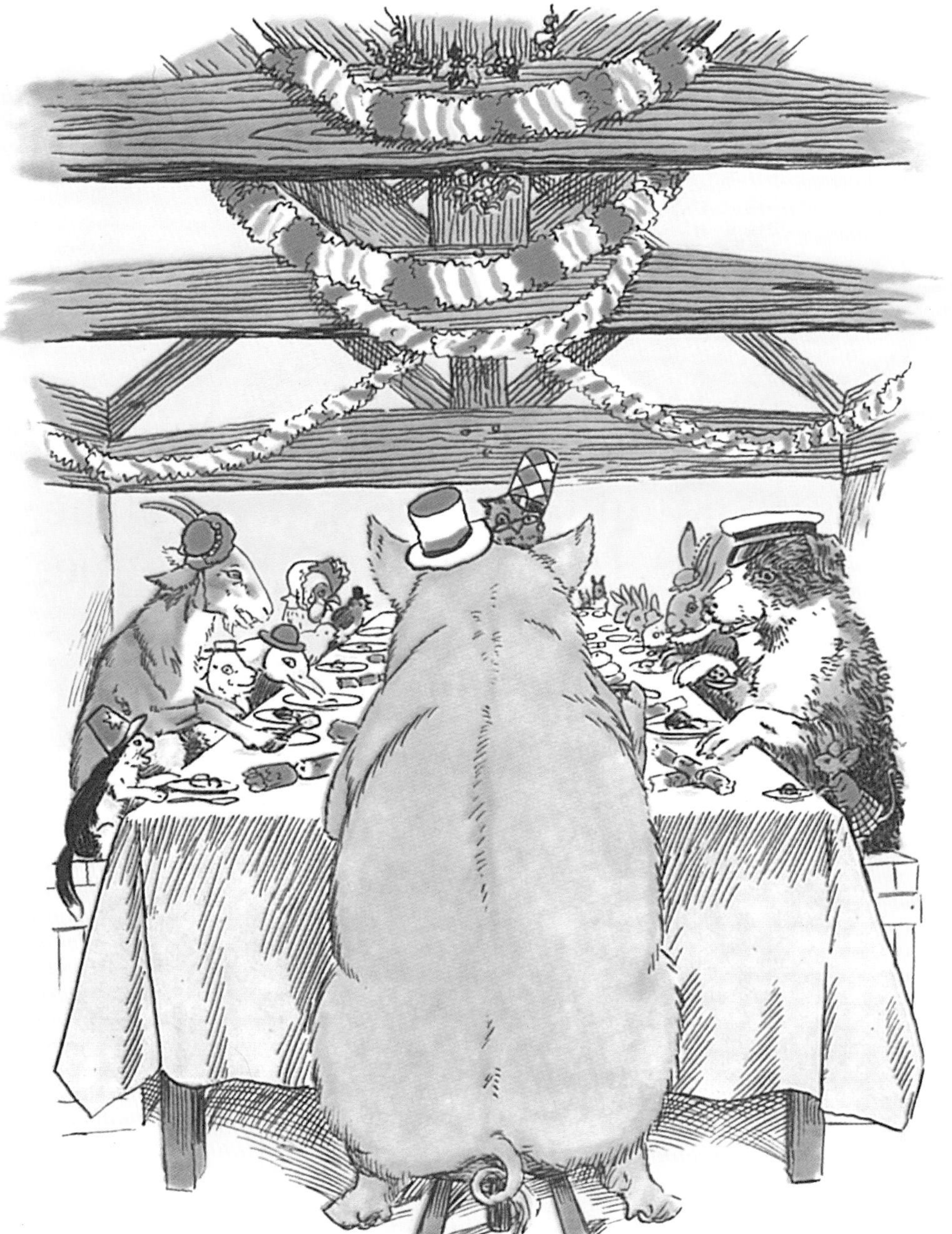

When they had eaten as much as
they could, and had pulled all the
crackers and tried on all the paper
hats, they lay down, full and
happy, and slept until tea-time.

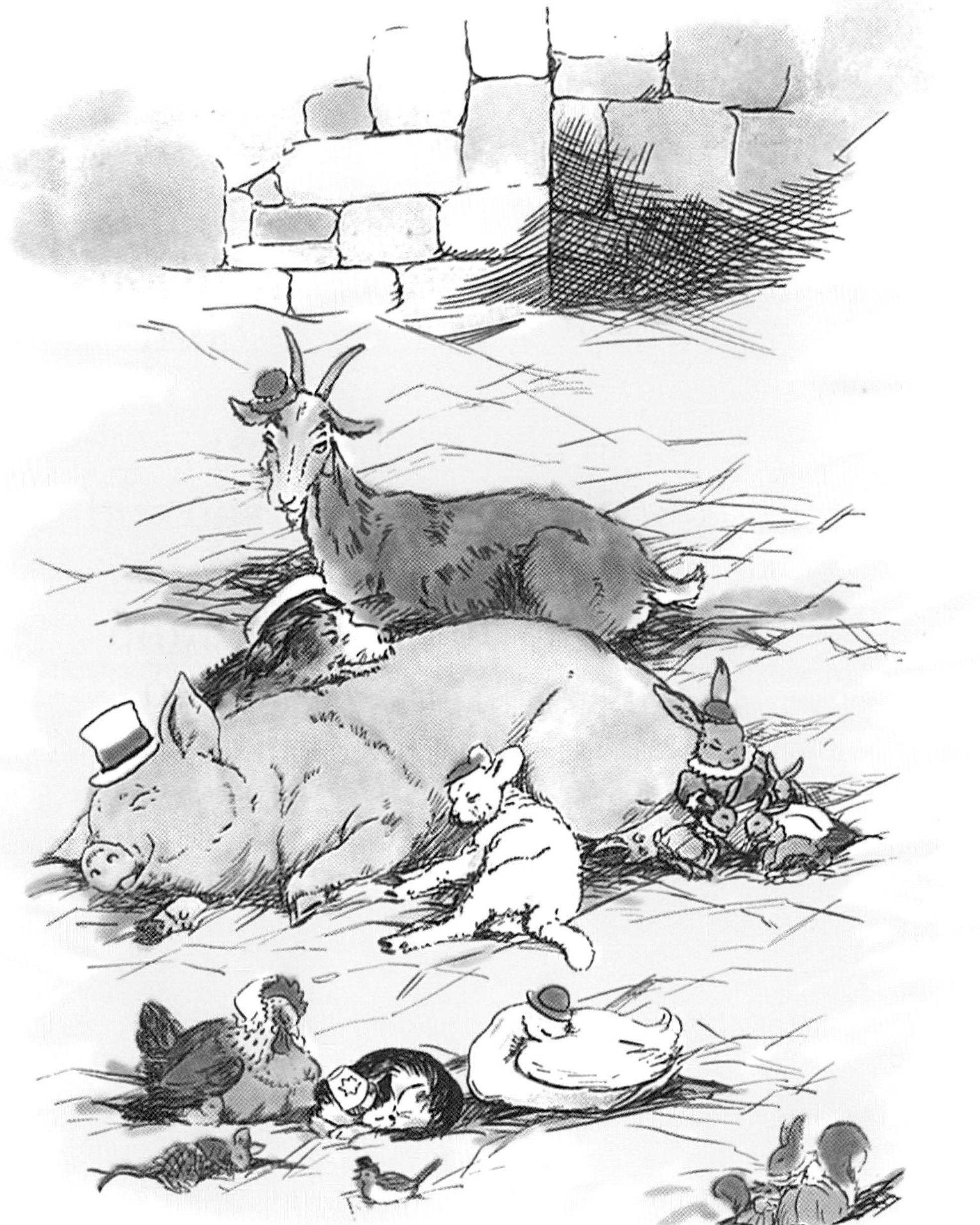

Then Mr and Mrs Smiles, with Joy and Bob, came down to the barn and lit the candles on the big Christmas tree, and Mrs Smiles cut the big Christmas cake she had made. They all played "Here we come gathering nuts in May" and "Ring-a-ring o'roses," and sang carols round the Christmas tree until it was time to go to bed.

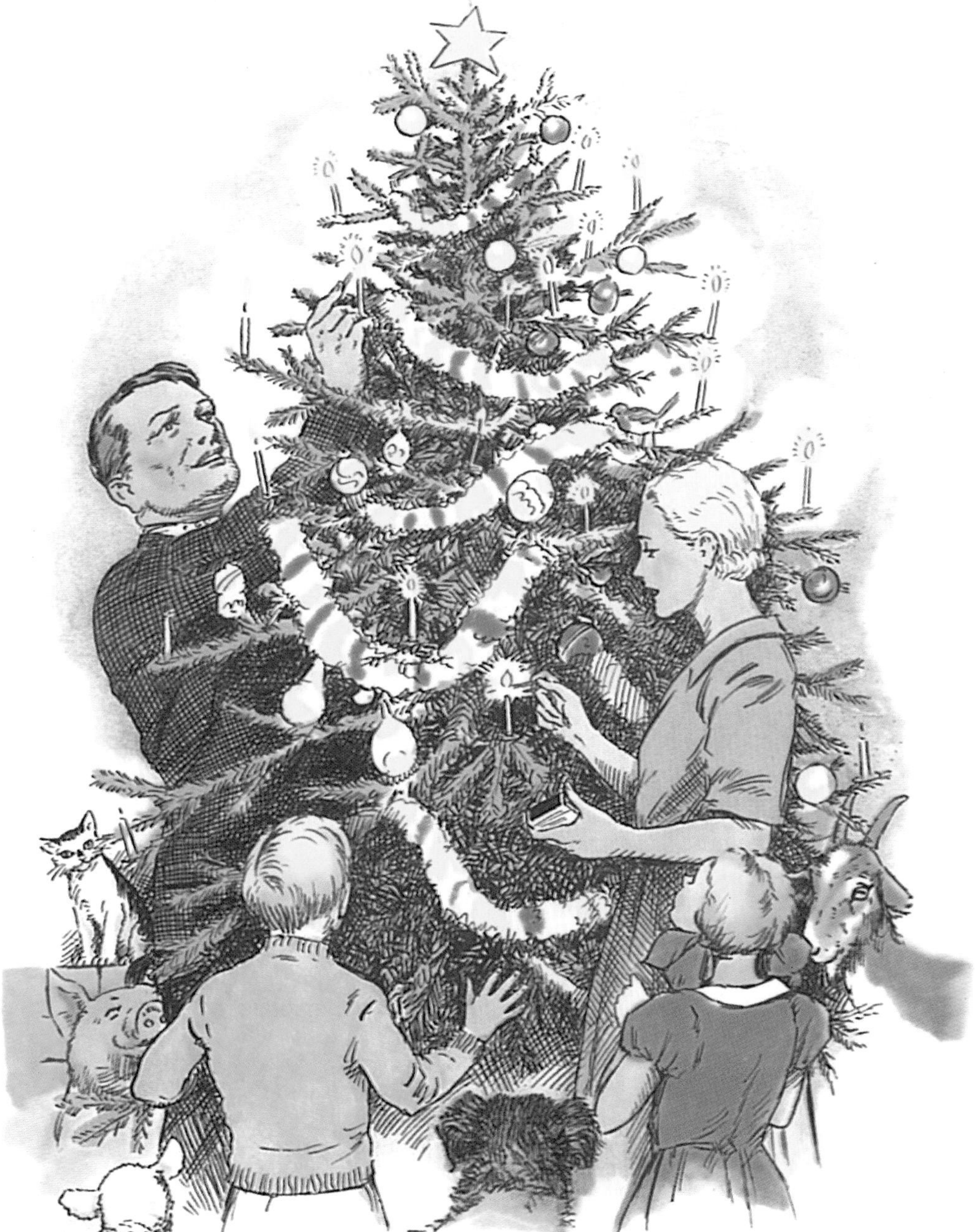

Then, tired and happy, the animals all said good night to Mr and Mrs Smiles, and thanked them for a lovely Christmas Day and trotted off to bed. And Joy and Bob said: "Thank you, Mummy and Daddy, for giving us all such a lovely time!" Mr and Mrs Smiles kissed them both, and said it had been one of the happiest days they had ever had at Blackberry Farm.

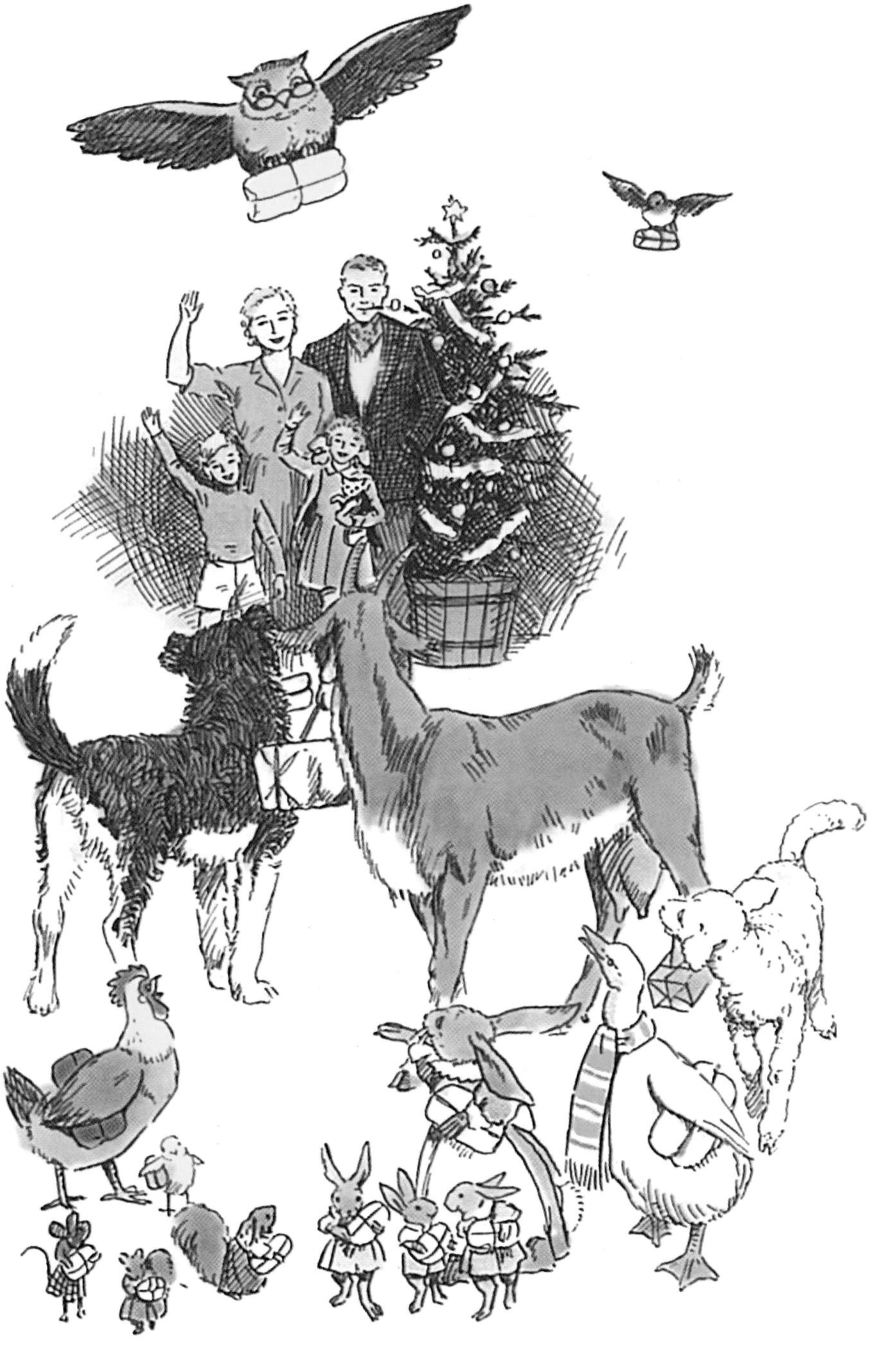